Giant Octopus to the Rescue

adapted by Alison Inches
based on a teleplay by Ligiah Villalobos
illustrated by Art Mawhinney

Ready-to-Read

Simon Spotlight/Nickelodeon
New York   London   Toronto   Sydney

Based on the TV series *Go, Diego, Go!*™ as seen on Nick Jr.®

SIMON SPOTLIGHT
An imprint of Simon & Schuster Children's Publishing Division
1230 Avenue of the Americas, New York, New York 10020
© 2009 Viacom International Inc. All rights reserved. NICK JR., *Go, Diego, Go!*, and all related titles, logos,
and characters are trademarks of Viacom International Inc. All rights reserved, including the right of
reproduction in whole or in part in any form.
SIMON SPOTLIGHT, READY-TO-READ, and colophon are registered trademarks of Simon & Schuster, Inc.
Manufactured in the United States of America
First Edition
2 4 6 8 10 9 7 5 3 1
Library of Congress Cataloging-in-Publication Data
Inches, Alison.
Giant octopus to the rescue / adapted by Alison Inches ; based on the teleplay by Ligiah Villalobos ;
illustrated by Art Mawhinney.
—1st ed.
p. cm.—(Go, Diego, go! ; #10)
"Based on the TV series Go, Diego, go! as seen on Nick Jr."—T.p. verso.
ISBN-13: 978-1-4169-6876-4
ISBN-10: 1-4169-6876-8
I. Villalobos, Ligiah. II. Mawhinney, Art, ill. III. Go, Diego, go! (Television program) IV. Title.
PZ7.I355Gid 2009
[E]—dc22
2008006782

Hi! I am  .
DIEGO

Today we need to rescue

some ocean !
ANIMALS

The  are trapped in
ANIMALS

CORAL

at the bottom of the ocean.

The is next to some

CORAL

underwater .

VOLCANOES

The  are getting

VOLCANOES

ready to blow!

We need an ocean animal to show us the way to the .

CORAL

 says the animal we need

CLICK

has **8** arms.

EIGHT

Is the animal a , a ,

SEA STAR   SQUID

or a ?

GIANT OCTOPUS

Count the arms to find out.

Which animal has **8** arms?

EIGHT

Right! We need a  !
GIANT OCTOPUS

We have to go under water

to find the  .
GIANT OCTOPUS

We can use my Rescue
 to find the .

SUBMARINE

GIANT OCTOPUS

To the rescue!

There is the  GIANT OCTOPUS .

The  GIANT OCTOPUS says he will

help us.

Hurry! We have to follow

the  GIANT OCTOPUS !

Look! The 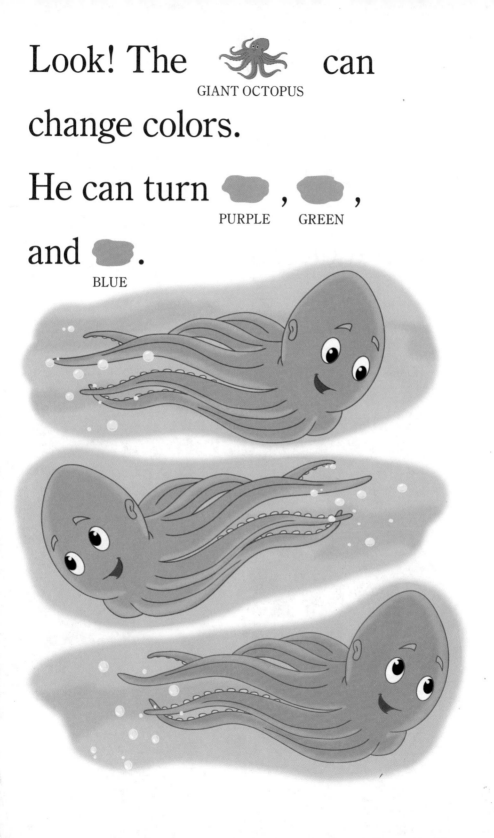 GIANT OCTOPUS can change colors.

He can turn ⬤ PURPLE , ⬤ GREEN ,

and ⬤ BLUE .

Oh, no! I see some .

WHALES

The  is afraid of !

GIANT OCTOPUS

WHALES

The  can squirt

GIANT OCTOPUS

PURPLE

ink to hide from the .

WHALES

The  cannot see past

WHALES

the ink, so the

PURPLE   GIANT OCTOPUS

can swim away.

Squirt, , squirt!

GIANT OCTOPUS

Watch out for falling  !
ROCKS

The ocean  will hit
ROCKS

my  .
SUBMARINE

The  can catch
GIANT OCTOPUS

the  .
ROCKS

How many 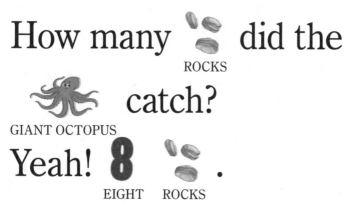 did the

ROCKS

 catch?

GIANT OCTOPUS

Yeah! **8** .

EIGHT   ROCKS

I see the  !
VOLCANOES
Do you see the trapped ?
ANIMALS

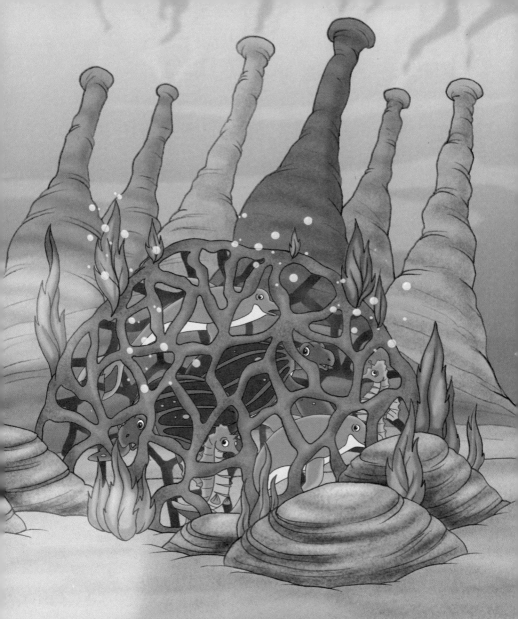

There they are!

The  GIANT OCTOPUS can use
his 8 EIGHT arms to dig a hole
under the CORAL .

Dig, , dig!

GIANT OCTOPUS

Now the 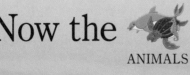 can swim to safety.

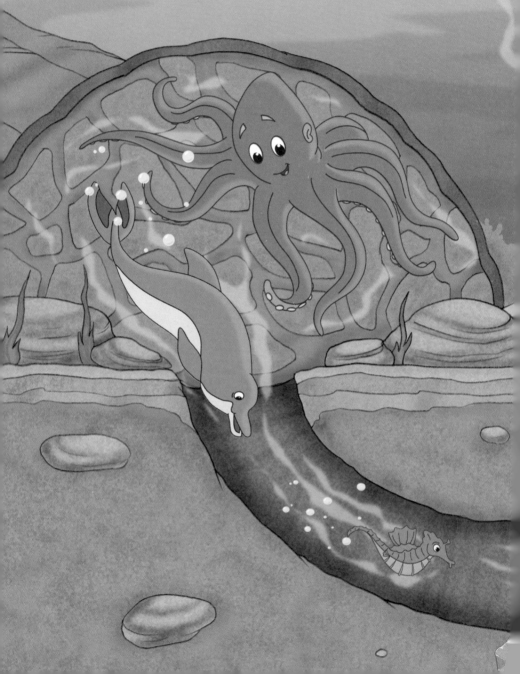

Swim, 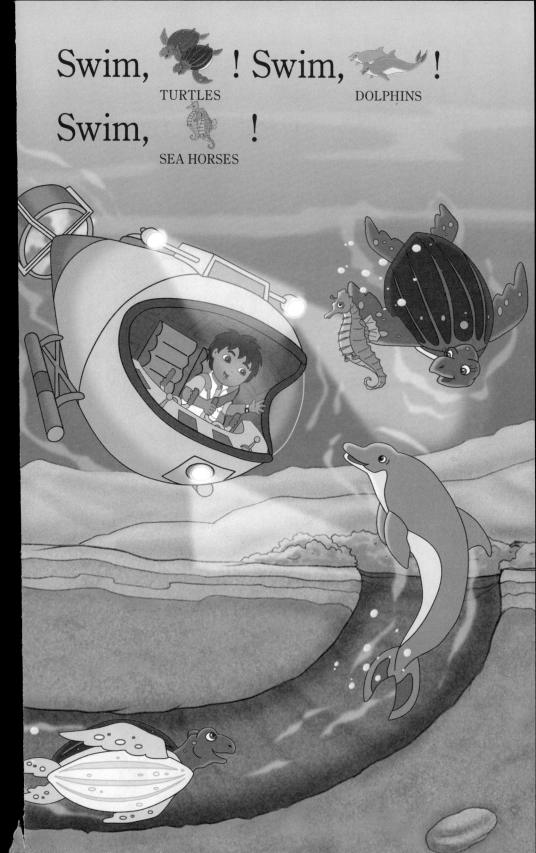 ! Swim, ! Swim, !

TURTLES

DOLPHINS

SEA HORSES

The ocean  ANIMALS are safe.
The VOLCANOES are about to
blow!

That was a **blast**!

You were a big help, and so

was the  .
GIANT OCTOPUS

Rescue complete!